THE Pattaconk Brook

James Stevenson

THE Pattaconk Brook

Greenwillow Books · New York

CURR
PZ
7
.S84748
Pat
1993

FRANKLIN PIERCE
COLLEGE LIBRARY
RINDGE, N.H. 03461

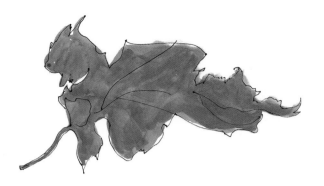

Down from the meadow where birch trees are leaning,
Down from the wildflowers yellow and blue,
Down through the dark green, wet, moss-covered boulders,
Over gold pebbles, past giddy ferns waving,
Plunging and pitching, tumbling and shivering,
The quick brook says, "Pattaconk, Pattaconk, Pattaconk."
The quick brook says, "Pattaconk," as it heads for the sea.

Sidney the green frog sat down on the brook bank,

Listened to the Pattaconk spatter and slap.

In a blue-lined black notebook he wrote down the sounds:

Thub cada bup

Go gul lop ulk

Aw cuh cuh lumb

We dee oh picka

Bip

Sherry the brown snail came slithering slowly.

She peered at the sounds that the frog had put down.

"You haven't quite caught it," said Sherry politely.

"You've missed quite a few of the sounds of the brook."

"Well, maybe," said Sidney, "you should get your own notebook

In which you could stick all those sounds I don't hear."

"I'm sorry," said Sherry. "Didn't mean to disturb you."

"That's all right," said Sidney. "It's tough trying to listen.

Perhaps you should tell me the ones that I've missed."

Sherry the snail slid her shell to the water.

She stretched out her neck and tilted her horns.

"Ooba du globum," said Sherry to Sidney.

"Ooba du globum—that's one that I hear."

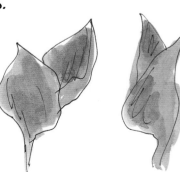

Sidney looked at his notebook. "I don't think I have that.

How do you spell it? I'll put it right down."

"I'm a listener, not a speller," said Sherry to Sidney.

"Whatever you put will be perfectly fine."

Ooba, wrote Sidney.

"Du globum," said Sherry.

Ooba du globum, wrote Sidney the frog.

Sherry and Sidney then sat there in silence,

Listening for sounds that the other might hear.

"I wonder," said Sidney, "what the Pattaconk sounds like

Down where the Pattaconk meets with the sea?"

"I haven't a clue," said the snail a bit sadly.

"There's no way to get there for slitherers like me."

Suddenly Sidney said, "Hey! I've been thinking.

A branch floating by might be jumped on and ridden.

One might ride over waterfalls down to the sea."

"Of course!" cried the snail.

"We could ride down the Pattaconk, glide down the Pattaconk,

Slide down the Pattaconk, down to the sea!"

When a branch from an oak tree came drifting downriver,

Sidney cried quickly, "This might be the one!"

He put down his notebook, his blue-lined black notebook.

"I'll carry you, Sherry," he said, "like a football."

He scooped up the brown shell and leaped to the oak branch.

With his free hand he grabbed an especially strong twig.

Then the branch caught the current and sailed like an arrow,

Shooting the rapids on the way to the sea.

"Hooray!" shouted Sidney. "Hang on for dear life!"

(From inside the shell he could hear a faint "Wheee!")

Then into the bubbles and over the gravel,

Racing round wet rocks, bobbing in foam,

Crashing through cattails and crossing thick grasses,

Splashing through dark pools, sliding through shallows,

Leaping off waterfalls into the air.

At last it got quiet. They could hear a bird singing.

The branch was now gliding through muddy green marshland.

"Sherry," said Sidney, "I think we've arrived."

The snail stuck her head out and looked at the landscape.

"My goodness," said Sherry, "I think we have, too."

When the branch bumped ashore at the end of the marshes,

They ran across mud flats and into a wood.

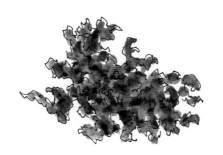

Hearing the thunderous thumping of ocean,

Smelling the sharp, salty scent of the sea,

Sidney took Sherry through bayberry forests,

Bullbrier tangles, wild cherry, and vines.

Breaking free of the jungle, they burst into sunlight.

Sidney—with Sherry—ran across the warm sand.

They slipped through wet seaweed heaped up on the shoreline.

They slid down the slopes of a mountain of kelp.

They splashed through the tide pools, past mussels and scallops.

They climbed over boulders where barnacles clung.

They ran up a steep dune where beach grass was bending.

Sidney was gasping when they got to the top.

"Aren't you exhausted?" said Sherry to Sidney.

"You must be quite tired from carrying a snail."

"No, snails aren't too heavy," said Sidney to Sherry.

"But maybe, for a moment, we might just sit down."

They sat on the dune, the breeze on their faces,

While sandpipers skittered, gulls glided above.

They listened to the thunder of giant waves falling,

The booming of surf from far down the shore,

The rattle of stones when the water retreated,

The hushing of foam fanning out on the sand.

"Good gracious," said Sherry. "These are better than brook sounds.

I never imagined such noises as these!"

A little while later a cold wind chilled Sidney.

"It's time," Sidney said, "to go back to our stream."

"I don't think I'm going," said Sherry to Sidney.

"Not going?" said Sidney. "You mean you'd stay here?"

"I've noticed," said Sherry, "there are snails every which way.

Many small creatures around here have shells."

"But what about the Pattaconk, the lovely green Pattaconk?

You can't leave the Pattaconk," Sidney declared.

"I have to," said Sherry. "I feel I belong here.

I know I'd be happy down here by the sea."

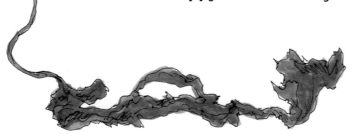

Sidney just sat. There was nothing to say.

"I'm sorry," said Sherry. "That's all right," said Sidney.

"You like where you're going. I like where I'm from."

Stretching his long legs, he said, "I'll be leaving.

My blue-lined black notebook is waiting for me.

I've heard many sounds down here by the ocean.

I'd better go write them before I forget."

"I'll miss you," said Sherry. "I'll miss you," said Sidney.

"But when the time's right, I'll come back again.

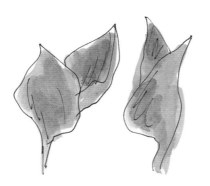 

"I'll jump on an oak branch and ride down the Pattaconk,

Glide down the Pattaconk,

Slide down the Pattaconk..."

"Down to see <u>me</u>?" said Sherry to Sidney.

"Exactly!" said Sidney, and then he was gone.

From the top of the sand dune, she watched him go hopping.

When he got to the forest, he turned back and waved.

Then a cherry branch trembled, a bayberry quivered.

Sidney the frog disappeared from her view.

Inching her way down the sand, she sang softly.

(Behind her, her trail slowly dried in the sun.)

"It's not like the Pattaconk, lovely old Pattaconk,

But I think I'll be happy

Down here

By the sea."

Watercolor paints and a black pen were used for the full-color art.
The text type is Seagull Light.

Copyright © 1993 by James Stevenson. All rights reserved.
No part of this book may be reproduced or utilized in any form
or by any means, electronic or mechanical, including photocopying,
recording, or by any information storage and retrieval
system, without permission in writing from the Publisher,
Greenwillow Books, a division of William Morrow & Company, Inc.,
1350 Avenue of the Americas, New York, NY 10019.
Printed in Hong Kong by South China Printing Company (1988) Ltd.

First Edition   10 9 8 7 6 5 4 3 2 1

Library of Congress Cataloging-in-Publication Data
Stevenson, James (date)
The Pattaconk Brook/by James Stevenson.
        p.   cm.
Summary: Sidney the frog and Sherry the snail follow
their brook all the way down to the sea, in search of
all the different noises it makes as it rushes along.
ISBN 0-688-11954-9.   ISBN 0-688-11955-7 (lib. bdg.)
[1. Rivers—Fiction.   2. Frogs—Fiction.
3. Snails—Fiction.   4. Sound—Fiction.]
I. Title.   PZ7.S84748Pat   1993
[E]—dc20   92-29404   CIP   AC

FRANKLIN PIERCE COLLEGE LIBRARY

00094533